The Courageous Children

Ayesha Abdullah Scott

The Islamic Foundation

More Islamic Books Available
www.kubepublishing.com

Copyright ©The Islamic Foundation 1989/1410H. Reprinted 2001

ISBN 978-0-86037-194-6
e-ISBN 978-0-86037-668-2

All rights reserved.
No part of this publication may be reproduced, stored
in a retrieval system or transmitted by any means whatsoever,
without the prior permission of the copyright owner.

MUSLIM CHILDREN'S LIBRARY
General Editors: **Manazir Ahsan** and **Anwar Cara**
Editing by: **Maryam Davis**

THE COURAGEOUS CHILDREN
Author: **Ayesha Abdullah Scott**
Cover design: **Anwar Cara**
Illustrations: **Ayesha Rahman**

These stories are about the Prophet and his Companions and, though woven around
authentic ahadith, should be regarded only as stories.

Published by
The Islamic Foundation, Markfield Dawah Centre,
Ratby Lane, Markfield, Leicestershire LE67 9RN, UK

Quran House, PO Box 30611, Nairobi, Kenya
PMB 3193, Kano, Nigeria

British Library Cataloguing in Publication Data
Scott, Ayesha Abdullah
   The courageous children
   1. Islam
   I. Title II Rahman Ayesha
   297
    Typesetting: LiteBook Prepress Services
    Printed by: Akcent Media

MUSLIM CHILDREN'S LIBRARY

An Introduction

Here is a new series of books, but with a difference, for children of all ages. Published by the Islamic Foundation, the Muslim Children's Library has been produced to provide young people with something they cannot perhaps find anywhere else.

Most of today's children's books aim only to entertain and inform or to teach some necessary skills, but not to develop the inner and moral resources. Entertainment and skills by themselves impart nothing of value to life unless a child is also helped to discover deeper meaning in himself and the world around him. Yet there is no place in them for God, Who alone gives meaning to life and the universe, nor for the divine guidance brought by His prophets, following which can alone ensure an integrated development of the total personality.

Such books, in fact, rob young people of access to true knowledge. They give them no unchanging standards of right and wrong, nor any incentives to live by what is right and refrain from what is wrong. The result is that all too often the young enter adult life in a state of social alienation and bewilderment, unable to cope with the seemingly unlimited choices of the world around them. The situation is especially devastating for the Muslim child as he may grow up cut off from his culture and values.

The Muslim Children's Library aspires to remedy this deficiency by showing children the deeper meaning of life and the world around them; by pointing them along paths leading to an integrated development of all aspects of their personality; by helping to give them the capacity to cope with the complexities of their world, both personal and social; by opening vistas into a world extending far beyond this life; and, to a Muslim child especially, by providing a fresh and strong faith, a dynamic commitment, an indelible sense of identity, a throbbing yearning and an urge to struggle, all rooted in Islam. The books aim to help a child anchor his development on the rock of divine guidance, and to understand himself and relate to himself and others in just and meaningful ways. They relate directly to his soul and intellect, to his emotions and imagination, to his motives and desires, to his anxieties and hopes – indeed, to every aspect of his fragile, but potentially rich personality. At the same time it is recognized that for a book to hold a child's attention, he must enjoy reading it; it should therefore arouse his curiosity and entertain him as well. The style, the language, the illustrations and the production of the books are all geared to this goal. They provide moral education, but not through sermons or ethical abstractions.

Although these books are based entirely on Islamic teachings and the vast Muslim heritage, they should be of equal interest and value to all children, whatever their country or creed; for Islam is a universal religion, the natural path.

Adults, too, may find much of use in them. In particular, Muslim parents and teachers will find that they provide what they have for so long been so badly needing. The books will include texts on the Qur'an, the Sunnah and other basic sources and teachings of Islam, as well as history, stories and anecdotes for supplementary reading. The books are presented with full colour illustrations keeping in view the limitations set by Islam. To capture the imagination of the child and to test his comprehension of the stories, a set of questions is given at the end of the story. Each book is designed to cater for a particular age group, classified into: pre-school, 5–8 years, 8–11, 11–14 and 14–17.

We invite parents and teachers to use these books in homes and classrooms, at breakfast tables and bedside and encourage children to derive maximum benefit from them. At the same time their greatly valued observations and suggestions are highly welcome.

To the young reader we say: You hold in your hands books which may be entirely different from those you have been reading till now, but we sincerely hope you will enjoy them; try, through these books, to understand yourself, your life, your experiences and the universe around you. They will open before your eyes new paths and models in life that you will be curious to explore and find exciting and rewarding to follow. May God be with you forever.

And may He bless with His mercy and acceptance our humble contribution to the urgent and gigantic task of producing books for a new generation of people, a task which we have undertaken in all humility and hope.

M. Manazir Ahsan
Director General

CONTENTS

		page
Introduction		7
1.	'Umair's love for Islam	10
2.	Mu'adh ibn 'Amr and Muawwidh ibn 'Afra	15
3.	Rafi' and Samurah	21
4.	'Umair the slave boy	26
5.	Salamah and the bandits	31
6.	Zaid ibn Thabit	36

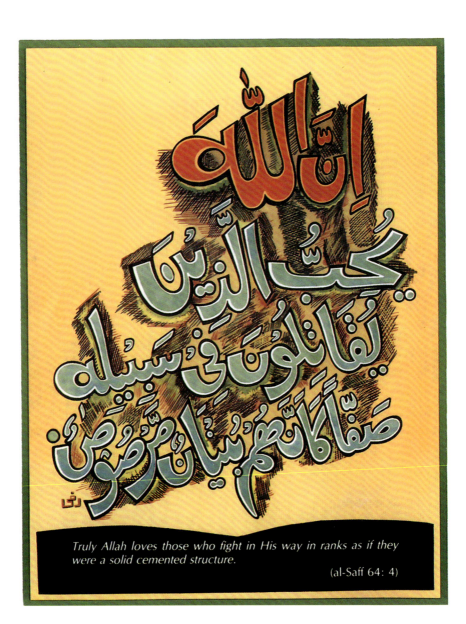

Introduction

When the. Prophet Muhammad (peace and blessings of Allah be upon him),* was ordered by God to tell the people that they should worship only the One God and that he was His Messenger, the people of Makka were very angry. For centuries they had worshipped idols. They had seen their fathers, their grandfathers and their priests worship the idols, so they were not ready to give up their familiar practices and accept Islam. Very few people in Makka accepted the command to submit to God alone, and believed in the Blessed Prophet Muhammad as God's Messenger. Though the Blessed Prophet was known as a man who always spoke the truth, most of the people refused to listen to him.

The Blessed Prophet was a very patient man. He continued to invite the people to accept Islam. When the number of believers started to increase, the unbelievers were furious. They beat and tortured the believers, yet the believers refused to give up their faith in the One God. They would rather die than accept the idols as their Lord. Gradually more and more people accepted Islam. The unbelievers increased their torment and the Muslims' suffering continued unabated.

---

* Muslims are required to invoke Allah's blessing and peace upon the Prophet whenever his name is mentioned.

When the torment showed no sign of lessening, the Blessed Prophet told some Muslims to migrate to Abyssinia. During this time, though the Blessed Prophet and the believers suffered all manner of ill-treatment from the unbelievers, they endured everything with patience and fortitude. The unbelievers even put a boycott on the Muslims. No-one was allowed to buy anything from them or sell anything to them. For more than two years, the Muslims suffered this hardship. Many of them had hardly anything to eat or wear. When eventually the unbelievers lifted the boycott, the Blessed Prophet told some of the Muslims to migrate to Madina, where they would be welcomed and could practise their faith. The Blessed Prophet continued to invite people to worship the One God. Finally, the unbelievers, desperate to stop the spread of Islam, decided to kill the Blessed Prophet. However, God ordered the Blessed Prophet to go to Madina.

For more than thirteen years, in Makka, the Blessed Prophet and the Muslims had suffered cruelty and ill-treatment at the hands of the unbelievers. They had patiently endured the violence and torture in the constant belief that God would help them.

When the Blessed Prophet arrived in Madina, many people there accepted Islam. The Muslim community gradually expanded and the first Islamic state was established with the Blessed Prophet as its leader. When the Muslim community grew strong, God gave them permission to fight against all those who prevent people from submitting to God.

The unbelievers' hatred for the Muslims deepened. They looked for any excuse to attack the Muslims in Madina. On the false pretext that one of their caravans was under threat near Madina, they gathered together a great army to attack the Muslims. The Blessed Prophet with only a few hundred followers met the Makkan unbelievers near Badr during the month of Ramadan. The Muslims won a glorious victory against those who had persecuted and tortured them because of their belief. To struggle in this way for the cause of Islam is known as Jihad. Jihad generally means effort and struggle in the way of Islam. Jihad has different stages; the highest stage is war against the oppressor which in Arabic is called Qital.

In this book, you will read stories of youngsters who were eager to join the Blessed Prophet to fight against the oppressor.

Questions:

1. Why did the unbelievers beat and torture those who accepted Islam?
2. What was the response of the believers to the sufferings caused to them by the unbelievers?
3. What are the aims of Jihad?

1
'Umair's love for Islam

'Umair ibn Waqqas wanted to join in the Muslims' fight against their enemies. He was not really old enough, but when he saw hi elder brother Saad preparing his camels and his armour ready to fight he just could not resist the urge to go along to help defend Islam.

At that time, the Muslims, under the leadership of the Blessed Prophet, were setting up the first Islamic State in Madina. The unbelievers in Makka did not want a strong community there which obeyed the One and Only God, Allah. They were determined to destroy the new faith of Islam which was growing stronger every day.

The unbelievers in Makka were always looking for an excuse to attack the new Muslim community in Madina. They found just the excuse they wanted when Abu Sufyan, chief of the Quraysh, was leading a caravan of 1,000 camels bringing valuable goods back to Makka from Syria. Abu Sufyan, suspecting that the caravan might be attacked by the Muslims as it passed near Madina, sent a message to Makka saying that they were already under attack and needed help. The Makkans quickly mustered a thousand men and marched on Madina.

The Blessed Prophet discussed this unexpected situation with his

Companions. Although they could only raise 313 poorly-armed Muslims, they decided to set off towards Makka to face the Makkan army before it reached Madina. Saad was one of that small group of believers. And, hidden away amongst the marchers, was his young brother, 'Umair.

'Umair knew full well that the Blessed Prophet did not allow young boys to fight with the Muslim army. But, praying that he would not be spotted before the battle began, he had taken his sword and slipped quietly in amongst the soldiers.

When the army halted, it was Saad who noticed an anxious-looking 'Umair. 'What are you doing here? Why are you hiding like this?', he asked. 'I want to fight for Allah', explained 'Umair. 'I love Allah and the Blessed Prophet so much that I am quite prepared to die for Islam. But if the Blessed Prophet catches sight of me I know he will send me back home. He will say I am too young. I have to fight without him knowing I am here.' Saad left 'Umair where he was.

Just as 'Umair had feared, the Blessed Prophet noticed him when he was lining up his soldiers. He told 'Umair that he was too young to fight and he would be sent back home to safety.

When the Blessed Prophet had walked away 'Umair burst into tears. He was heart-broken. His sobs attracted the attention of some soldiers standing nearby. 'How bitterly disappointed young 'Umair must be to be sobbing like that!', they exclaimed. They

discussed 'Umair's plight among themselves. Then, they decided to go and tell the Blessed Prophet about it.

Upon hearing how distressed 'Umair had been because of his decision, the Blessed Prophet remained silent for a few minutes. Then, with a smile, he granted permission for 'Umair to join the Muslim army.

When 'Umair heard the news he could hardly believe it. His tears changed to smiles. When the soldiers left for Badr, where the battle was to take place, 'Umair marched along proudly with the rest of the soldiers.

Just before the battle started Saad noticed that 'Umair's sword was dragging along the ground. It was far too big for him. Saad shortened the straps of the sword-belt so that 'Umair could manage the sword more easily.

In those days, whenever two armies wanted to fight, they would first call the champions from both sides to single combat. After that, others might take the place of the champion who had been killed or wounded. Then would follow the command for the whole army to proceed for the fight. The battle of Badr started in the same way.

The Muslim army advanced on the Makkans chanting 'God is One, God is One'. 'Umair was only armed with a single sword, whereas the Makkan army were well armed with sword and shield. Many of the Makkans were mounted on horses and camels during the fight. 'Umair was not scared of the enemy. The desire to die for the cause of Islam kept him fighting to the last breath. He inflicted many death blows on the enemy. He was wounded in the battle but never stopped fighting. He carried on till he was martyred by 'Amr ibn 'Abd of the Makkan army.

The battle ended with the victory of the Muslim army over the Makkans. Many of them fled and some were taken prisoners. The Muslim army also suffered some losses. Fourteen Muslims died fighting for the cause of Islam and 'Umair was amongst them. He died a martyr, just as he had wanted, fighting to protect Islam from the oppressors and unbelievers, and thus he gained Allah's pleasure, and became one of the very young martyrs (Shahid) in Islam.

Questions:

1. What excuse did the unbelievers of Makka use to attack Madina?
2. Why did 'Umair want to join the Muslim army?
3. How did the battle start at Badr?
4. What happened to 'Umair and the Muslim army at Badr?

2
Mu'adh ibn 'Amr and Muawwidh ibn 'Afra

The early Muslims in Makka had many enemies but one of the most troublesome was a man called Abu Jahl. His name meant 'the father of ignorance'. It suited him well. He was arrogant, violent and cruel. When the leaders of the Quraysh met in Makka to discuss ways of silencing the Blessed Prophet it was Abu Jahl who suggested that each clan should choose a strong young man and that, at a given signal, all the young men should attack and kill him. In this way each clan would be jointly responsible for the Blessed Prophet's assassination.

The Angel Jibra'il brought a message to the Blessed Prophet warning him of this cruel plot. Allah commanded that he should leave Makka and join the small group of Muslims in Madina. But even when the Muslim community was being established in Madina the Muslims still suffered from Abu jahl's evil influence.

In the second year of Hijra, the Makkans marched with a big army towards Madina. At the head of a small and poorly-armed Muslim army, the Blessed Prophet set off towards Badr to meet the Makkans.

It was the month of Ramadan. The Muslim army were fasting and they had a very arduous journey ahead of them. At that time it was very hot and the sun was blazing down on the Muslims. Among the marchers were two young boys named Mu'adh ibn 'Amr and Muawwidh ibn 'Afra. The march was hard and tiring for them too. After two days of march, the Blessed Prophet ordered the Muslims to break their fast in order to prepare them physically for the very hard battle waiting for them ahead.

Before setting off to fight, Mu'adh ibn 'Amr and Muawwidh ibn 'Afra had sworn a pact that, with the help of Allah, they would find the hated Abu Jahl who was doing his best to destroy the Blessed Prophet and, when they found him, they would kill him.

When the Muslim army reached Badr, an oasis eighty miles from Madina, the Blessed Prophet Muhammad ordered them to occupy the well. The Muslim army set up camp and prepared themselves for the battle. The Blessed Prophet Muhammad had divided them into groups and gave them very important instructions about the Jihad which was going to take place. He told them that they should not kill women, children and others who are not armed for battle. They should not cut down trees or use torture against their enemy. The purpose of Jihad is not to take revenge but to fight against the oppressor for the cause of God.

Next morning the Muslim army were ready near the hills, waiting for the Makkans to advance. The sun was rising behind the hill and the rays of light struck directly in the eyes of the advancing Makkan army. When the Makkans saw that the well was occupied by the Muslims, they were forced to fight.

The two armies came face to face in battle on the seventeenth day of Ramadan. The two boys, Mu'adh ibn 'Amr and Muawwidh ibn 'Afra, were in the midst of the battle, fighting bravely for Islam. They kept looking for Abu Jahl among the enemy soldiers.

'Abdur Rahman ibn 'Awf who was fighting beside the boys noticed them all the time looking to right and left as if they were searching for someone. In a lull in the fighting he asked them who they were looking for. 'We have to find Abu Jahl', they replied. 'We are going to kill him.'

Soon afterwards 'Abdur Rahman spotted Abu Jahl: 'There he is!' The boys immediately ran over to where Abu Jahl was fighting. As he was on his horse they could not reach up high enough to attack him directly. So, Mu'adh ibn 'Amr struck at the horse's legs while Muawwidh ibn 'Afra rained blows on Abu Jahl's legs until, with a loud crash, both Abu Jahl and his horse tumbled down. They fought fiercely but Abu Jahl was stronger and more experienced at fending off blows. No matter how hard the boys struck him, they were only able to inflict small wounds.

Abu Jahl's son, Ikrimah, also joined in the fray, helping his father to ward off the boys' blows. He struck Mu'adh ibn 'Amr with his sword and almost severed his arm at the shoulder. As the battle was still raging all around them Mu'adh ibn 'Amr found himself moving away from Abu Jahl. He was fighting with his good arm while the other hung limply by his side. When the pain became too much for him to bear he severed his own arm and then resumed fighting.

Muawwidh ibn 'Afra carried on striking at Abu Jahl until there seemed to be no breath left in his enemy's body. Just then another Muslim who hated Abu Jahl passed by. 'Abdullah ibn Mas'ud had been the first man to recite the Qur'an aloud in front of the Ka'ba in Makka and Abu Jahl had struck him for it, wounding him in the face. He now grasped the opportunity to complete the job the boys had started and, with one blow of his sword, killed the man who had done his best to destroy Islam. Having carried out his promise to kill Abu Jahl, Muawwidh ibn 'Afra fought on against the unbelievers. During the fierce fighting he was killed. He gave his life for the cause of Islam and became a martyr for his devotion to Allah.

Questions:

1. What kind of person was Abu Jahl?
2. In what condition did the Muslim army march to Badr?
3. What was there in common between Mu'adh ibn 'Amr and Muawwidh ibn 'Afra?
4. What important things must a Muslim observe in the Jihad?
5. Describe how Mu'adh ibn 'Amr and Muawwidh ibn 'Afra were able to overcome Abu Jahl and what happened to them?

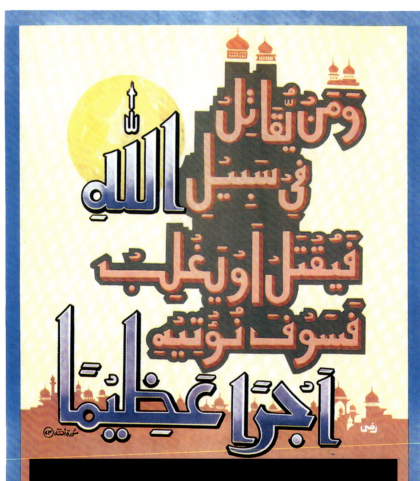

3
Rafi' and Samurah

The Battle of Badr had left the Muslims' enemies in Makka feeling very sorry for themselves. They could not forget how their thousand-strong army had been defeated by 313 ill-equipped Muslims who had even included young boys. They were determined to fight the Muslims again so that they could take revenge for this humiliation. They began to prepare for another attack on the Muslims.

Meanwhile, the Muslims in Madina were busy establishing their Islamic State. Their victory at Badr had given them fresh confidence. They had seen that strength comes from faith in Allah, and not from military might. One of the Blessed Prophet's uncles, 'Abbas, was a Muslim but he had not moved to Madina; he still lived in Makka. From there he was able to observe the unbelievers' military preparations and keep the Blessed Prophet informed.

When 'Abbas sent a message to Madina that an army of 3,000 troops was soon to leave Makka with 700 men in armour, 200 mounted on horseback and as many camels as men, the Blessed Prophet quickly gathered around him the Islamic community's elders to discuss the crisis.

The elders thought it would be best to defend Madina from inside the city but the younger men were eager to advance towards the approaching Makkans. They knew that martyrdom would be more easily gained if they met the Makkans outside, and they were ready to give their lives for Islam. As most of the men were in favour of fighting outside the city, the Blessed Prophet decided to go out and meet the Makkans.

Some boys, who were regarded as too young to fight, were also keen to join the army. If the Blessed Prophet saw them, however, he would send them back home.

Among the boys who wanted to fight were two close friends named Rafi' and Samurah. Although they were only boys they were skilled fighters. Rafi' was a good archer; he always beat Samurah in a contest. But Samurah was a skilled wrestler who always managed to beat Rafi' when they wrestled.

Half-way between Madina and Uhud the Blessed Prophet halted his army for Maghrib prayers, after which he inspected his troops. When he noticed a group of young boys who were hoping to fight he ordered them to return to the safety of their homes in Madina. Among the boys were Rafi' and Samurah.

Rafi''s father, Khadij, spoke up for his son: 'O Prophet of Allah, my son is a very good archer.' Rafi' stood on tiptoe to make himself look as tall as possible. He and his father waited with bated breath for the Blessed Prophet to make his judgement. Seeing how keen both Rafi' and his father were that he should be allowed to fight, the Blessed Prophet said that he could stay.

Samurah was very disappointed when he heard that Rafi' could join the army but he could not. Why must I go back home without having a chance to fight for the sake of Islam? he thought, but he did not say a word. Instead, he went to look for his step-father, Murayy ibn Senaan. When Samurah found him he complained: 'The Blessed Prophet has allowed Rafi' to fight but he has rejected me. I can beat Rafi' when we wrestle and I think I could have been chosen before him.'

When the Blessed Prophet was told what Samurah had said, he called both boys to his tent. On arrival they greeted the Blessed Prophet, saying: 'As salamu alaykum.' After being asked to enter the tent they sat down in front of the Blessed Prophet who turned to Samurah and gently questioned him: 'Is it true that you can beat Rafi' at wrestling?' 'Yes', said Samurah shyly. The Blessed Prophet smiled and said to Samurah: 'If you can beat Rafi' in a wrestling match I will let you stay with us, but if you lose you will have to go back to Madina with the other boys.'

Samurah's earlier disappointment turned to joy. He was happy because he was sure he could beat Rafi' and then he would be allowed to fight for Islam.

The contest began. The two boys circled around one another. The sun beat down on them. Samurah was determined to beat Rafi'. They fought keenly but fairly. Although Rafi' fought well, he was not quite so skilful as Samurah. At last, after a hard contest, he had to admit defeat.

Samurah was thrilled. Now the Blessed Prophet would allow him to fight in the coming battle. And Rafi' was happy because his friend would be beside him in the battle, Fighting together for Islam was far more important than losing a wrestling match.

Questions:

1. Why did the unbelievers attack Madina again and how strong were they?
2. What did the Blessed Prophet do when he received the news that the unbelievers were about to attack Madina again?
3. Why did Rafi' and Samurah want to join the Muslim army?
4. What contest did the Prophet organize for Rafi' and Samurah and why?
5. Imagine yourself to be Rafi' or Samurah. Express your joy on being allowed to fight for Islam.

4
'Umair the slave boy

'Umair was a young slave boy. Although he was small for his age he was very strong and brave. His good behaviour and hard work pleased his master who was called Abil-Laham.

'Umair loved to learn about Islam. He was always looking for ways to please Allah and the Blessed Prophet, who was living in Madina at that time. The one thing that really excited 'Umair was the thought of Jihad. It was his greatest wish to defend Islam against the unbelievers who were always making trouble for the Blessed Prophet and his followers.

'Umair was certain that if the trouble-makers could be defeated the Muslims would be able to live in peace and to spread the message of Islam far and wide. Ever since the Blessed Prophet had started to preach the message that Allah was revealing to him in Makka he had faced fierce opposition from the unbelievers. The wealthy merchants had turned against him because their trade depended on people coming to Makka to worship the idols in the Ka'ba. They ill-treated and tortured the Muslims so much that eventually the Blessed Prophet sent some of the believers to Madina for safety.

After thirteen years in Makka preaching belief in the One God and suffering abuse from the unbelievers, the Blessed Prophet was finally commanded by Allah to migrate to Madina and join the small community of local Muslims and his followers from Makka. But even in Madina the Makkans and the Jews would not let the Muslims live in peace. After a further two years of ill-treatment Allah granted the Muslims the right to defend themselves by Jihad against their enemies.

'Umair liked the idea of pleasing Allah through Jihad. He was very excited when, hard at work for his master one day, he heard that the Blessed Prophet had decided, in accordance with the divine command, that the time had come to fight back against the Muslims' enemies. The unbelievers of Makka who still refused to accept the Blessed Prophet's message had joined forces with the Jews in Madina. The Blessed Prophet had to expel from Madina some of the Jews who had caused trouble and they had moved to Khaibar. From Khaibar the Jews and the unbelievers had started plotting together to kill him.

When 'Umair heard that the Blessed Prophet was preparing to go to Khaibar he immediately wanted to accompany him. But he knew that it was unlikely that his master would release him. Even if he was allowed to go he did not think that the Blessed Prophet would allow him to fight. 'Umair was very worried about this until he suddenly thought: If it is Allah's Will that I should fight, then I will fight. Why am I worrying like this?

'Umair rushed to his master Abil-Laham and pleaded with him to release him and to ask the Blessed Prophet to let him fight for Islam at Khaibar. Abil-Laham saw in 'Umair's eyes a genuine, deep desire to fight for Islam. He knew what an obedient, brave boy 'Umair was, and what a great love he had for the Blessed Prophet. Abil-Laham knew then that he could not refuse to do as 'Umair asked.

'Yes, I will release you and I will also ask the Blessed Prophet to allow you to go to Khaibar', he told 'Umair. 'But I do not know whether he will give his permission for such a small boy as you to fight.' 'Umair had to wait patiently for an answer.

Abil-Laham greeted the Blessed Prophet with Salam and then explained why he had come. He fold the Blessed Prophet all about 'Umair and his deep love for Allah. He described 'Umair's eagerness to fight although he was still so young and he spoke of his bravery, his strength and his good character.

The Blessed Prophet agreed to let 'Umair accompany him to Khaibar. 'Umair was overjoyed when he heard, but then his face clouded over as he realized he had another problem. He did not have a sword. 'How can I fight without a sword?', he said to himself. 'Now that I have permission to fight, I haven't anything to fight with!' He felt very miserable as he wondered how he could get a sword. He had no money to buy one. What could he do?

When the Blessed Prophet noticed 'Umair's troubled face he smiled and handed him a sword. 'Umair's heart pounded with excitement as he took it. The Blessed Prophet himself had given him a sword! Now he really would be able to defend Islam. He thought it was the most magnificent sword in the world. He did not care that it was

really too big and heavy for him. He just hung it around his neck and let it drag along behind him.

In the Battle of Khaibar 'Umair fought bravely and the Muslims were victorious. After the battle, the Blessed Prophet ordered that everything captured in the battle should be shared equally among the Companions. 'Umair knew that he was too young to receive a share. In any case, being allowed to fight alongside the Blessed Prophet was reward enough for him. But the Blessed Prophet had been so impressed by 'Umair's desire to join in Jihad that he gave him a share of the booty as a special reward.

So, 'Umair, though only a young boy, proved to be a brave fighter for Islam.

Questions:

1. Why did 'Umair want to fight for Islam?
2. Why were some of the Jews expelled from Madina and what did they do afterwards?
3. Why did Abil-Laham seek permission from the Blessed Prophet for 'Umair to join the Muslim army?
4. What was 'Umair's reward after the Muslim army won the battle?

5
Salamah and the bandits

During the early days of Islam, there were many bandits roaming around. They often raided the Muslim community which was trying to live peacefully in Madina.

One leader of a group of unbelievers who had become a bandit was Uyaynah al-Fazari. He and his followers caused the Muslims many problems. One day, they decided to steal the Blessed Prophet's camels. They knew that the camels were taken to graze at the small village of Ghaba, just outside Madina.

The bandits hid and watched the Muslims bring the Blessed Prophet's camels to the village. They waited patiently until the men and boys were on their way back to Madina, leaving behind just one man to look after the camels. Then, they jumped onto their horses, shouting wildly, and started to run off with the camels. The Muslim who had been watching over the camels drew his sword and tried to fight off the bandits. Although he fought bravely he was outnumbered by the bandits who killed him before setting off back to their camp with the camels.

As the bandits were leaving, a twelve-year-old boy out on the hills spotted them. This boy's name was Salamah bin Akwa'. He was one of the best archers amongst the Muslims in Madina. He was also a good runner and could outrun not only boys but men as well. They said he could run as fast as a horse.

Salamah was devoted to the Blessed Prophet and constantly tried to please him. Now he had a golden opportunity to help him by trying to save his camels. He rushed to the top of a hill overlooking Madina, shouting loudly to some Muslims who were working outside the town. 'Hurry! Hurry! Bandits have taken the Blessed Prophet's camels.'

Without waiting for help Salamah turned back to chase the bandits by himself. Running as fast as his legs could carry him, he caught up with the bandits who had no idea that he was behind them. Staying out of sight, he began to fire arrows at them. He fired the arrows so rapidly that the bandits thought that there were many Muslims chasing them. While he was shooting Salamah prayed: 'O Allah! Please do not let them find out that I am here all alone.'

The bandits were surprised and frightened by the sudden attack and started to make off without the camels. They did not want to face the anger of the Muslim leader when he found out what they had done.

Just then the chief of the bandits, Uyaynah al-Fazari, arrived to help his men and saw that Salamah was alone. 'Hey', he shouted after the bandits. 'You are not afraid of this one young lad, are you?'

The bandits were very angry when they discovered that Salamah had tricked them. They decided that death was the best punish-

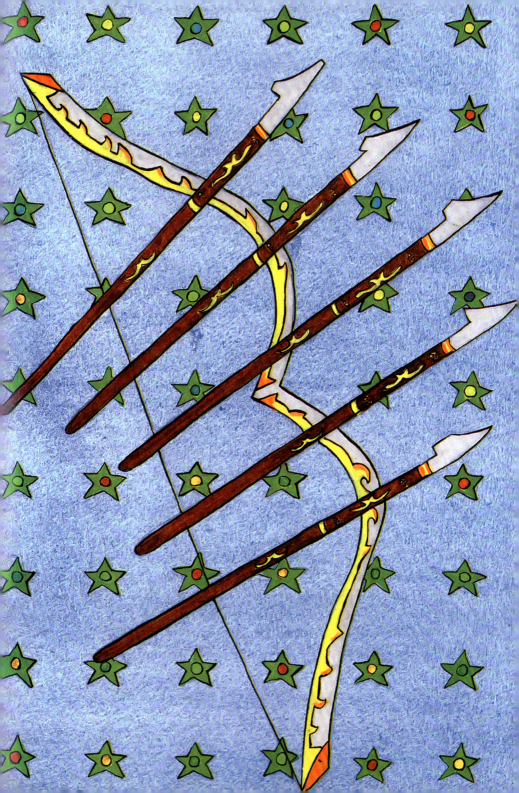

ment for him. They forgot all about the camels as they rode off to catch Salamah who was already making his escape. But, though they rode their horses at a fast gallop they could not catch him. With increasing fury they chased Salamah into the hills near Madina. He ran up the slope with the bandits racing along close behind him. His heart was pounding as he dived into a clump of trees near the top of the hill. Hiding behind a tree he started shooting arrows at the bandits.

Salamah kept the bandits at bay with his well-placed arrows. He thought, If I can only hold on for a little longer, our soldiers will surely come to help me. Then he began to taunt the bandits. 'Stop!' Salamah shouted. 'Listen to me! Do you know who I am? I am the son of Akwa'. By Him Who has given glory to the Blessed Prophet, if any one of you chases me, you will never catch me. But if I run after any one of you, you will not be able to escape from me.'

These taunts angered the bandits even more. They were so angry that they thought only about catching young Salamah. Salamah waited anxiously for help to arrive. He knew he could not keep the bandits at bay for much longer. Minutes seemed like hours to him.

Then, the Muslims who had come to help Salamah rode into the midst of the bandits and some fierce fighting followed. A few bandits managed to escape but many were killed. Only one Muslim lost his life.

When Salamah saw the Blessed Prophet he asked: 'Can I have your permission to chase the rest of the bandits? I would like to bring them back to take their punishment.' The Blessed Prophet smiled at Salamah, and said: 'No Salamah, there is no need for that.'

Salamah had already shown how brave and intelligent he was, and that was enough. After all, this young boy had saved the Blessed Prophet's camels by tricking the bandits into believing that there were many Muslims attacking them.

Questions:

1. Why did the bandits want to steal the Blessed Prophet's camels?
2. What did Salamah plan when he saw the bandits stealing the Blessed Prophet's camels?
3. What did the bandits do when they discovered that Salamah was alone!
4. What happened to the bandits when the Muslims came?

6
Zaid ibn Thabit

Zaid ibn Thabit was only six years old when his father died, leaving him an orphan. At the age of eleven he went to Madina where he stayed with the Blessed Prophet whom he grew to love above all other people. He soon knew that he wanted to spend all his time helping the Blessed Prophet to spread the message of Islam.

At that time, the Muslims in Madina were surrounded by enemies who refused to believe in Allah, the One God. Earlier, when they were living in Makka, the Muslims had been constantly persecuted by the leaders of the powerful Quraysh tribe who did not want people to believe in Allah. Their persecution of the Muslims reached such a pitch that Allah commanded the believers to leave Makka and settle in Madina where they hoped they could find peace.

In Madina, the Makkans continued to harass the Muslims. Zaid realized how important it was to spread Allah's message to the unbelievers so that more of them would turn to the right path, and join the Muslim community. Zaid was among those chosen by the Blessed Prophet to write down the verses of the Qur'an whenever Allah revealed them to him. Zaid spent much of his time, each day, learning by heart the words of Allah. Each time the Blessed Prophet received a new revelation Zaid learnt it as quickly as he could. Naturally, when the Makkans started to attack the Muslim community in Madina with the intention of destroying the new faith, Zaid was anxious to become a soldier so that he could help to defend Islam.

The first major attack by the Makkan army resulted in the Battle of Badr. Zaid wanted to fight in this battle although he was barely twelve years old. When the Blessed Prophet turned him down because he was so young he was extremely disappointed. Although he was upset, he was not discouraged. A year later he volunteered again to fight at Uhud where 700 Muslims were facing a 3,000-strong Makkan army, but once again the Blessed Prophet shook his head, saying: 'No. You are too young. Stay behind in Madina where you will be safe.'

Zaid felt very sad after this second rejection. He found comfort in reciting the Qur'an and he continued to learn all the messages that Allah revealed to the Blessed Prophet. His intelligence and love of learning were so well recognized that when the Blessed Prophet was looking for someone he could trust to write his letters, he chose Zaid. To be secretary to the Blessed Prophet Zaid had to learn both the Hebrew and Syriac languages.

Zaid again volunteered to fight when he was nineteen years old. This time the Blessed Prophet accepted him for the Muslim army. Zaid was delighted; at last he had the opportunity to fight for Islam. He still found time to learn each of Allah's revelations and

to recite the Qur'an, even while he was preparing for the forthcoming battle.

Zaid's time to fight had come nine years after the Blessed Prophet established the Muslim community in Madina. Makka had been taken over by the Muslims the previous year. When news reached the Blessed Prophet that the Byzantine empire had mustered an army to invade Arabia, he decided to assemble an army and march to meet the threatened attack. The Blessed Prophet sent orders to Makka and the allied tribes for them to send all their available armed and mounted men to Madina to accompany him.

As the contingents of men arrived a large camp grew up outside Madina. Eventually the army was 30,000 strong with 10,000 mounted men. The Blessed Prophet then took command of the vast army and led the march towards Tabuk. Each contingent had a flag; it was a great honour to be chosen as a standard-bearer in the Muslim army. Proudly bearing the flag of one tribe, the Bani Malik, was a man named Amarah.

When the Muslim army had marched only a short distance, the Blessed Prophet approached Amarah and asked him to give the flag he was carrying to Zaid ibn Thabit. Amarah could hardly believe his ears. 'Why?', he asked himself. 'Zaid is far too young to have the honour! I must have done something to upset the Blessed Prophet. Someone has complained to him about me.'

To the Blessed Prophet Amarah said sadly: 'O Prophet of Allah, are you doing this because someone has been complaining about me?'

'No', replied the Blessed Prophet. He smiled gently at Amarah: 'It is because Zaid knows more of Allah's revelations than you. It is his knowledge of the Qur'an which gains him preferential treatment.' Reluctantly, Amarah handed over the standard to Zaid.

Zaid was overjoyed to receive this great honour from the Blessed Prophet. He carried the flag throughout the expedition of Tabuk. It made up for all his earlier disappointments. The Blessed Prophet demonstrated that age and fighting experience alone do not make a good Muslim soldier. A love of Allah and knowledge of the Qur'an are just as important, or even more so. Zaid accepted that as well as being able to fight for the sake of Islam he must continue to memorize the whole of the Qur'an.

Questions:

1. Who was Zaid ibn Thabit and what was his wish?
2. What responsibilities did the Blessed Prophet give to Zaid ibn Thabit?
3. How did Zaid ibn Thabit feel when he was not granted permission to join the Muslim army?
4. What honour did the Blessed Prophet give to Zaid ibn Thabit?